POINT OF VIEW

Point of View

Peyton M McElravy

Artist Credit

The cover art was masterfully illustrated by Zainah. They can be found on Instagram and Artistree at the same name.

Dedication

I would like to dedicate my novella to many more people than I can name. I have been influenced so much through the stories these people have told in novels, tv shows, movies, plays, musicals, games, etc. that I can never possibly attribute them all. However, the one I believe has influenced me the most is Brennan Lee Mulligan. The stories that he has told alongside the intrepid heroes, and many others have kept me company throughout the highs and lows of my life and even right now as I write this. I thank you all for making my imagination strong enough to survive this world, and I hope that one day I can do the same for others with the stories I plan to tell.

Contents

1

Approaching Storm

" Lord Wyllran calls for an audience! All staff, residents, and visitors of the keep are to assemble in the ballroom within the hour!"

The voice sounded a bit frantic and anxious, but that was to be expected. At least in the opinion of the visiting scribe, Harbin Yklan. He was a young man with quite handsome features who wore a simplistic yet well-crafted pair of dark trousers, a grey tunic buttoned all the way to the top, and a fur-lined red coat embroidered with the golden spiral designs often seen upon the clothing of House Yklan scribes.

He hadn't been quite so interested in the visit to this Lord's home since it was just another journey to copy documents and carry them back to the House's main branch to be preserved. However, an unforeseen circumstance had occurred.

Harbin looked down toward the boy announcing the Lord's will to the keep's residents. The boy was on the ground floor of the manor while Harbin himself was atop the staircase leading to the indoor balcony area of the second floor. From here, Harbin could see the boy's youthful features; he himself couldn't be much older than the boy, possibly only 4-5 years, placing the boy at a mere 15 or 16. It was too much pressure to place a task such as announcing the Lord's word upon the shoulders of such a young man.

He must also be worried about the upcoming announcement. Harbin, however, had been in the room when Lord Wyllran received word about the impending snowstorm, so he wasn't as alarmed or curious as the other residents within the manor.

Still, he would be required to attend the meeting regardless if he already knew the announcement, and so he began making his way to the ballroom as directed. The halls themselves were gorgeously crafted in Harbin's opinion. The deeply dark wood walls were illuminated by the soft candleglow of the beautiful silver wall sconces, allowing all of the wood's texture to be revealed, even though they were nearly as dark as the wood itself. The ceiling rose high into marvelous arches, nearly fifteen feet high.

The floors were all individually crafted marble mosaics depicting the historical triumphs of House Yklan. Some showed the battlefield whereupon the founder of House Yklan won his knighthood, some showed the founder's descendants fighting horrible beasts and monsters, and some depicted Lord Wyllran himself. In most, he rode atop his noble steed, a chestnut colored horse outfitted with all the amenities of a pampered ceremonial mount. Harbin eventually looked up from the marvelous scenes beneath his feet and took in the sight of the crowded entryway to the ballroom instead.

Being located at the center of the keep made most residents have an almost equally long journey to its marvelously carved doorways, causing a halt in the progression of its occupancy.

While waiting, Harbin took a moment to look upon the doors themselves. They appeared to be made of the same dark oaken wood as the halls and rising from their surface was a carving that depicted a knight in full armor with a sword stabbed into the ground in front of him. Soon after the crowd was alleviated from its bottleneck, Harbin looked away from the doors and entered into the room, and soon after him, the Lord arrived within the ballroom as well. Standing high above the currently bare room was a small balcony area that looked over the ballroom, directly emerging from the Lord's chambers in the central spire, somewhere above the cavernous space.

Servants hastily ran throughout the room. Some lightning candles, some holding tall silver handled torches, and some placing down seats for the high nobility who resided within the keep. The ballroom itself was far from its usual beauty as this was a rather hasty gathering called together by the Lord, however the largest and most eye-catching feature came into view in all its usual glory. This feature was the large fireplace along one of the walls, shadows of dragons began being cast upon the wall as it began to roar with fire. Normally, such a thing might be odd in a ballroom; however, this keep was located pretty far north in the world, making the location quite prone to the cold.

After the room was thoroughly glowing with warm candlelight, the Lord spoke. His voice was low yet not menacing, similar to the stern voice of a father figure. Harbin quickly pulled open his tome of blank parchment and a bit of sharpened charcoal to take notes on this speech; he was here to be a scribe after all.

"Attention!" The anxious crowd grew silent quickly. "As some of you may already know, a large snowstorm is swiftly approaching."

The crowd whispered among themselves for a moment, and some relieved sighs ran throughout the room as their worry for greater danger swiftly turned to curiosity at the Lord's next words.

"Our dedicated scholars have predicted that the incoming storm will likely trap us within the keep itself for the next 2 days..." The Lord paused for a moment to let the words reach the ears of his people. "We have enough within our stores to keep everyone fed and relatively comfortable, so you do not have to worry about such things during this time period."

The people gathered seemed to grow a little excited, especially the non-residents, since normally they would only work within the keep during the day and return to their own homes in the evening. In addition, opportunities to eat food fit for nobility was a rare occasion for these people.

"However, you will all be expected to fulfill your duties as you normally do to the best of your ability. Our keep may become our prison for a small while; however, it does not need to look like one."

That last remark received a small chuckle from the assembled crowd, especially from the nobility seated within a section of the ballroom all their own.

"Those of you who do not have rooms will be given a small cushion and a blanket from our Head Butler, Mr. Leidan Mor, and then assigned a space here within this very ballroom." The Lord spoke with a well-practiced authority.

"Dinner will be prepared within the kitchen starting in one hour, eight o'clock, and soon after, you will all be asked to remain in either your rooms or within your assigned sleeping space." The Lord continued.

"Hmm, that's odd." Harbin began to think to himself. *"Why would he be confining us?"*

Harbin glanced up from his writing and carefully looked toward the Lord.

He couldn't see much from where he stood; however, he managed to catch the eye of the Lord himself. Apparently, seeing him writing, the Lord gave a small, nearly imperceptible nod in his direction.

"Perhaps he wishes to make sure no one attempts to venture out into the cold?" Harbin thought to himself once more.

Soon after the Lord's speech concluded, the space exploded into motion. Most of which came from the staff who now needed to prepare sleeping arrangements and food for the couple hundred assembled new temporary residents of the keep.

2

Evening Respite

Harbin was one of the first to leave the ballroom as he didn't want to end up caught behind the crowd once more as they began to swarm toward the banquet hall. Soon after he found himself in a rather familiar yet empty hall, headed toward a small set of stairs hidden partially behind a well-carved pillar. He had always preferred to take the staff's halls and stairways within other nobility's homes for a few reasons.

One of these reasons was just that they were much more efficient. He often didn't have time to navigate the large and opulent rooms and halls of the proper residence, however the serving staff's halls led just about everywhere, and while they could be a bit maze-like at times, they were often much more direct. The other reason was that the serving staff was simply much more honest than the nobility they worked for. In this particular keep, Harbin could name at least a dozen nobles who had treated him with thinly veiled disrespect in the form of lies and insults within his first hour, excluding Lord Wyllran, of course.

Following the snake-like passageway that he had already memorized this morning, Harbin managed to come to a small door built into the wall of a particular hall. This hall was the one just underneath where the Lord's chamber itself was. Lord Wyllran had given Harbin the use of one of the higher-end guest chambers within the keep. It was one of only three other rooms on this floor. Two of the other rooms were guest chambers, currently occupied by Lady Ilya (the Lord's cousin) and Lord Vikar (the Lord's uncle). Each of them was of a higher status than the lord himself and were visiting on behalf of the Yklar family's head, Lord Wyllran's father, and Lord Vikar's brother.

The last room was a study for the lord. He often used it to display his various books, however it was mainly used to host a few of his closer friends for after-dinner drinks. Currently, it was being used as Harbin's main space to transcribe Lord Wyllran's business documents and other important documents.

Harbin soon found himself lying down within a large four-poster bed with a small candle on the bedside table, softly glowing in the otherwise darkened room. He laid his tome on the table beside him and looked at the ceiling above him. He silently wondered what the Lord was doing in that large chamber of his. Perhaps he, too, was preparing for the night's slumber and the days ahead.

*knock *Knock *Knock

"Hmm, I wonder who that might be?" Harbin thought to himself.

He got out of his large bed and crossed the opulently decorated room's length with the small lit candle in his hand, illuminating his surroundings. Soon, he arrived at the large double doors and opened one of them slightly to find the timid and anxious-looking boy who had announced the meeting about two hours before.

"Does the Lord need something?" Harbin asked in a slightly curious tone. Perhaps the lord wished for his audience specifically.

"No, sir," The boy responded quickly. "I was simply told to bring this to you. It is from the head butler, Mr. Mor."

Harbin looked down for the first time at what the boy was holding. In his hands was a small silver tray with a note and a small container of what appeared to be tea resin.

"Thank you," Harbin responded with a smile as he looked at the boy's face.

"Of course, sir." The boy responded as he nearly dropped the tray he was holding, attempting to both hand over the things on top of it and simultaneously keep it aloft.

Harbin caught the edge of the tray and grabbed the whole thing himself before saying in a slightly comforting tone. "You must be quite nervous with all of the duties the Lord and Mr. Mor have assigned you."

The boy let out a slightly strained smile before responding, "I am, sir. It has been most challenging yet rewarding work!"

The boy pulled on his collar for a moment before Harbin spoke once more with a comforting smile on his features. "They do not choose people for this job lightly young man, the very fact you have been selected is a testament to your character. I believe you will be quite alright in time."

The boy shyly smiled and bowed his head before bidding farewell, leaving Harbin to his own devices once more.

After a moment, Harbin walked over to a small hearth attached to one of the rooms in the chamber, letting a small pot of water begin to warm over the flame. He sat down on one of the comfortable armchairs near the fire and began to read the note Mr. Mor had sent, curious about its contents.

"Dear Mr. Harbin,

I have been made aware that you did not receive your dinner this evening. As the head butler of this keep, I cannot allow a scribe such as yourself go without any sustenance this night, and so I have sent along some tea. It is from the land of Darrogh, where the night is cold beyond belief. I hope it will keep you warm this evening and hold you over until the morning.

-Mr. Mor, Head Butler"

Harbin looked over at the small silver box next to him and picked it up. As he opened it, he was immediately hit with the scent of fir trees and something a bit sweet. Not more than a few minutes later, Harbin sat silently in his comfortable armchair by the fire and sipped the tea. It was smooth and slightly bitter; he felt as though he could fall asleep right then and there as a pleasant warmth spread through his bones. But, he decided against it and went to make his way to his large and extravagant bed.

Not even taking a candle on his way back this time, he blindly walked back to the bed with a keen sense of direction. On his way, however, he passes by the small silver tray from earlier on a nearby desk. It was faintly illuminated by the somewhat distant flame from the other room, allowing Harbin to see his own face within it.

He hadn't shaved the day before and had grown a little stubble, but for the most part, he still looked like his usual handsome self. Smiling for a moment, he turned away from the mirror and began to walk toward his bed.

But.. Just for a moment, he could swear his face within the silver tray...lingered for a moment.

"No, I must be too tired, and I've begun to see things." Harbin comforted himself. *"Also, low candlelight is said to induce hallucinations."* He continued within his own thoughts. He was a rather educated individual and prided himself on knowing facts like these. Soon, the siren call of his bed lulled him into it's embrace, and he quickly fell into a pleasant slumber.

3

The First Encounter

What felt like only a few moments later, Harbin was awoken to the sudden sound of a scream echoing down from the staircase leading to the Lord's chambers above.

"AHHHHAAH, GET OUT OF—"

The scream seemed pained, like the Lord was being attacked by some sort of assassin.

Harbin shot out of bed faster than he meant to, losing his balance and finding himself on the floor.

"*What the-?*" He thought to himself as his eyes adjusted to the low light.

He began to realize that there was something off with his vision; his surroundings swam and swirled through his eyes as if they were multicolored streams of water.

"*Have I been drugged?*" Was his first thought. However, his second was a lot more pressing. "*Lord Wyllran!*"

Harbin stumbled his way toward the antechamber to his chamber and grabbed a firepoker from beside the flame that had long since burned out. Using it as a cane, he eventually found himself among others quickly heading up the staircase toward the Lord's chambers.

The door to his rooms appeared to be locked by the looks of Mr. Mor at the head of the group, seemingly fumbling with a ring of silver keys.

Acting quickly, Harbin located the servants' entrance within the hallway and entered into the narrow corridors, finding it quite difficult to navigate due to his present state.

After a few minutes, the voice of Mr. Mor could be heard from somewhere below, "Call the guards! Break the door down!"

Some time later, Harbin found himself at the servants' entrance within the central chamber of the Lord's rooms.

"You fiend!" A hushed but agitated voice sounded from the inside, seemingly coming from the Lord. "You will not take me this night! Nor any night for that matter!"

Then, a cold chill seemed to crawl over Harbin as he pressed his ear against the door.

"I will, you wretch." The voice was eerie and surprisingly calm. It was as if whatever 'fiend' this was had no hellish passion or intent, simply calculated truths. But there was something else to it that Harbin couldn't quite place…

"I am that which haunts your mind, Lord Wyllran." The cold voice continued, "That mind of yours…how much more of me can it handle? Before… It… Breaks?"

"*That voice…*" Harbin thought hard for a moment as he listened. "*Its tone seemed to say its will was inevitable and nothing could stop it, yet at the same time, the core of its voice was… stoic, deep, assuring, masculine…was it perhaps…the voice of a Lord?*"

Harbin swallowed hard as he pushed back the fear sprouting in his heart.

Carefully and slowly, he reached his hand for the small metal handle of the door…

*creeeeaaaak

"*Damn!*" Harbin thought before he suddenly threw open the door! Only to see the Lord standing alone in the middle of the room dressed in his evening wear.

The two stared at each other for a moment. Confusion and panic on the face of Harbin…

Complete and utter fear on the face of Lord Wyllran...

4

A Chilling Voice

Standing completely still in the central room of the opulent bechambers stood it's owner, Lord Wyllran, and one other figure, Harbin the scribe.

"Lord Wyllran.. Who were you—?" Harbin's question was cut short as a loud bang erupted from the room to the pair's right.

"Search the room!" The familiar voice of Mr. Mor roared into the room. "My Lord, are you alright!?" He continued as he caught sight of Lord Wyllran.

Harbin turned his attention back to Lord Wyllran, still confused about the situation. Had the Lord been looking at that mirror just a moment ago? The fear that had been upon his features just moments before was replaced by a comforting smile and apologetic expression. "Mr. Mor, I am glad you have come so quickly–"

Harbin's swimming vision suddenly shifted as he found himself violently flung to the stone floor.

"ACK–" Was all the noise that could escape from his mouth before he realized his attacker was one of the guards that had made their way into the room. The man had taken the butt of his spear and slammed it into his back, then with his armored foot, he kicked away the fire poker.

"*Why are they...!?*" Then it hit him. He was the only other person visible in the Lord's chambers after he had screamed; he was holding a metal fire poker and was visibly disoriented. *They think I'm the attacker!*

"Wait–!" A fist slammed down into his jaw. He felt a tooth dislodge near the back of his mouth.

Mr. Mor walked over with a powerful gait, considering his age. "Why have you come to attack the Lord, boy!?"

Harbin looked at Lord Wyllran standing in the background of this tumultuous scene, pleading with his eyes for him to explain what really happened. Lord Wyllran stepped forward and placed a firm hand on Mr. Mor's shoulder.

"Mr. Mor, show some kindness." With his other hand, he made a motion to the guard holding Harbin down, and soon he was allowed to get up.

With much difficulty, Harbin managed to stand, only falling once. As he finally rose to his feet, Lord Wyllran spoke once more. "Mr. Mor, this young man is no attacker or threat."

A wave of relief washed over Harbin, allowing him to finally feel the rapid heartbeat in his chest.

"He must have indulged too much in beverages within his room this evening; it's quite obvious due to his condition."

"*What?*" Harbin thought to himself before the Lord continued.

"He must have had some sort of delusion about some rival of his and stumbled his way to this room, assuming that I was that person."

"What? No, I–" Harbin started before he was interrupted.

"Silence, boy!" Mr. Mor spoke with anger and odd disappointment in his voice still.

"Mr. Mor, I have urged you to act with some kindness. After all, this was just a misunderstanding." Lord Wyllran gently reprimanded, "I myself misunderstood at the beginning as well, believing him to be some sort of assailant or thief!"

Mr. Mor looked down for a moment before meeting the eyes of the Lord, receiving a small nod in return. "Alright, my Lord. Guards, escort Scribe Harbin back to his chambers, assure he is to have no access to anywhere else in the keep until he has regained his senses."

"Of course, sir!"

Then Harbin's mind suddenly went blank for a moment as he caught the eye of Lord Wyllran. He shook it off as he glanced around the room, only to find himself with a closed fist extended outward toward Mr. Mor, who now had a bleeding lip.

"*What is happening!?*" Harbin panicked within his mind.

Holding a piece of cloth to his mouth, a furious-looking Mr. Mor promptly called out. "Guards, take him away!"

"What, I didn't–" Harbin pleaded.

"You have struck my head butler, young Harbin," Lord Wyllran suddenly came into view. "This I cannot excuse."

The Lord motioned to the guards, who once again threw him to the floor, however this time they tied his hands together with a bit of coarse brown rope. They then lifted him to his feet and began shoving him toward the door, presumably toward the dungeons.

"After I had already begun sending him on his way..." Mr. Mor's voice could be heard over the murmuring people crowded near the doorway. "Despicable."

Harbin wrestled his head around back toward the open doorway and looked within, meeting the gaze of Lord Wyllran. All those gathered were staring at Harbin as he was being escorted out, the only person at the back of the crowd being Lord Wyllran, who met his gaze with a deep sadness and guilt. Completely different from his behavior just a few minutes before.

Within the hour, Harbin found himself in a cell somewhere beneath the keep. Three walls of damp stone, and one of cylindrical black metal bars. It appeared as if this one was separated from the rest at the very back of the large prison. As he was thrown onto the hard ground, he soon found that the weather outside has made this cell much colder and more inhospitable than it would've been before.

"Here's a blanket, you drunkard." The guard said in a disgusted tone as a thin wool blanket hit him in the face. Soon after that the guards locked the cell door and left, leaving Harbin alone with his thoughts.

"What just happened?... Someone obviously framed me, and perfectly at that." He thought carefully over the events of the night before, concluding a few things. *"I was drugged, perhaps the tea? It was purposefully something that would disorient me, allowing whoever it was to perfectly engineer a condition in which I needed something to help me walk..."*

"They also would've had to make sure I was the only one able to get into the room...Mr. Mor was fumbling with his keys, perhaps one was stolen! This person would have had to have known I would use the servants' entrance as well. They must've been the same as the one in the room with Lord Wyllran before, only if they were, why would they have fled? And why would Lord Wyllran have lied about why I was there? And why did they sound exactly like Lord Wyllran as well? This person also must have made me hit Mr. Mor! They disappeared in mere moments, sounded exactly like Lord Wyllran, and somehow made me strike Mr. Mor? This person must have truly been a fiend! Or at least has magic befitting one!"

As his vision began to recover, Harbin found himself extremely tired. A side effect of the drug most likely. He believed that the events of the night would make him unable to go back to sleep; however, he found the opposite to be more likely. Soon after these thoughts, he had himself huddled against the back corner of the cell, wrapped in the blanket, and shortly after, he was fast asleep, allowing the first day stuck within the keep to truly come to a close.

5

Pieces of the Puzzle

Habin awoke to the sound of a slight metallic ringing in the early hours of the morning.

He looked upwards at the small barred window leading to the outside of the keep, seeing no morning sun shining through. His gaze soon fell upon the bars that made up the fourth wall of his dirty stone cell. A masculine silhouette soon found its way into his vision. Initially, he wasn't able to make out any details as a candle burning in the silhouette's hand provided a harsh bit of warm light to the room; however, after his vision adjusted, he realized that he recognized the figure. Standing before him was none other than Lord Wyllran.

"Stay quiet, young Harbin." The man said, carefully and with a hidden bit of emotion in his voice. Harbin noticed that the man's hands were covered in something resembling soot; the candlelight did not provide enough light to see much more.

"I do not see him nearby; however, I still can't be too careful." Lord Wyllran quickly put out the candle he was carrying in his hand, plunging the room into pitch darkness.

"Why have you done this to me, Lord Wyllran? Or was it this "him" you speak of?" Harbin responded, nearly silent with his questions.

The Lord heaved a quiet sigh, and while Harbin could not see the man due to the absence of light he felt as though Lord Wyllran was very tired.

"I cannot tell you specifics, even these words now are at the risk of your life." Lord Wyllran's voice got closer, and though Harbin could not see him in the darkness, he assumed the man had gotten very close to the bars. "You were framed, you know who has done it." After those words, Harbin could hear a rustle of clothing and then a dulled metallic clang as something hit the ground within the cell.

"Open it after I have left and prepare for tomorrow night. I have a plan, meet me in the ballroom." The Lord then took out a match and relit the candle in his hand before quickly moving out of the prison corridor and up into the main keep.

Harbin waited in the cell, and as soon as the dim light finally disappeared from the end of the stone passageway, he reached around blindly looking for whatever the Lord had dropped onto the ground of the cell. After a few moments, his hands and clothes were covered in dust from the less-than-maintained floor, and he was now holding a small object wrapped in a black cloth.

"*Is it...?*" Harbin thought to himself before carefully unwrapping the cloth. Inside was a large iron key, matching the metal that made up the bars of the cell. However, the key had apparently seen some damage. Harbin looked carefully over it and found that some sort of rough material was used to scratch up the key all over, and then it was quickly covered in some dark powder.

"*It is a key! But why is it like this? I assume the Lord himself did this; however, what is the reason?*" Harbin thought to himself silently as he pondered what to do in his cell.

"*I know who framed me...It must be whoever was talking to Lord Wyllran earlier this night, but why wouldn't he just say that? He seemed afraid that he would be overheard, and while he did speak more quietly, his main course of action was putting out the light. Perhaps the strange magic the other Lord has is somehow related to light? That doesn't seem very fiendish...*"

Faint sunlight began to fill the chamber as the morning light finally crested to the point that it could shine through the window. "*In any case, I cannot act until the sun goes down once more. Otherwise, I'll be caught before I even get out of this cell!"*

As Harbin silently thought about what he would do the following evening, another figure found its way to the front of his cell. This figure was smaller, slightly frail, and seemingly very anxious.

"Sir Harbin?" A familiar, young-sounding voice called.

It was the boy he had seen several times throughout the past day, that last time being when he was delivered the poisoned tea. "Why have you come to visit me, young man?" He asked with a slight bit of suspicion.

"I-I am not really sure who to inform of something that happened, sir. And, for some reason, I recall you being quite kind to me." The nervous boy spoke. A tremble could be heard in his voice, seemingly hiding some stronger fear.

"What happened?" Harbin prodded the boy to continue.

"Sir, I-I um." The boy took a moment to breathe before continuing. "I have been informed by Mr. Mor that you have been placed here for acting violently while in a drunken state. I was also informed by Mr. Mor that he thought it was incredibly despicable of you to do such a thing after he had sent me down to bring you some of his tea."

"Have you come down here just to inform me of how 'despicable' I am? Or does this insult have a question, boy?" Harbin said to the boy, anger and annoyance blooming within his heart.

"N-no, sir! I just...It took me by surprise when Mr. Mor said that because... I cannot remember bringing you tea last night!' The boy finally spat out as a look of intense anxiety and fear appeared on his face.

"*What?*" Harbin began to think back through last night's conversation with the boy. "What is your name, young man?"

"Thomas, sir."

"Very well then, Thomas. It does surprise me that you would not remember something that had happened yesterday; however, you have been put in many stressful positions recently, so perhaps you ju—" Harbin was cut off by the young Thomas.

"You don't understand, sir! I don't remember it. But I do it at the same time!" Thomas looked down at his palms and spoke once more as the gaze of a perplexed Harbin landed upon him. "I do not remember being given the tray or the message to deliver it to you from Mr. Mor at all! I just suddenly remember being in your doorway and seeing you look at me... I was so startled that I nearly dropped the tray that I was suddenly holding!"

"Young Thomas has a gap in his memory? Harbin thought to himself before lowering himself to look the boy in the eyes. "Thomas, what was the last thing you remember before finding yourself in my doorway?"

The boy thought hard for a moment before responding. "I-I think I remember being in the servants' corridors near Mr. Mor's office. I was looking at the clock."

"Tell me, Thomas, how long would it take to walk from that place to my doorway?" Harbin asked, a thought slowly forming in his mind.

"Well," The anxious boy looked down for a few seconds before looking back at Harbin. "A few minutes, I suppose? Why do you ask, sir?"

"A few minutes...Thomas was not himself..." The thoughts churned together as more and more pieces fit into place. *"I was suddenly not myself as well when I found my fist striking Mr. Mor, and Lord Wyllran was acting completely different from the way he was during the altercation last night as well! A few minutes after he started acting odd, he was suddenly looking at me with guilt! It must truly be that fiend! He has the powers of possession; however, they only last for a few minutes at most...So when Lord Wyllran yelled 'get out of my—' earlier in the night, he most likely wasn't going to say 'get out of my room' but 'get out of my head' instead!"*

Harbin sat silently for a few minutes, feeling the key within his pocket and contemplating what it all meant. Before long, he looked back up at Thomas in front of him. "Listen, Thomas, can you do something for me?"

He hesitated for a moment before nodding and allowing Harbin to continue. "I need you to return here just before the sun fully sets. Bring a small mirror, a dagger, one pouch of ash, and one pouch of soot with you."

"Of course, sir!" The boy responded, however, just before he turned around, he asked with fear in his voice, "Sir...do you know what really happened during the time I was not myself?"

Harbin let out a sigh before replying, "Yes. I believe you poisoned me, young Thomas."

The boy clenched his fist for a moment before scampering off down the hall.

6

Calculated Risk

The sun began to set over the cold stone interior of the underground cell. Harbin was wrapped tightly in his thin blanket, clutching the soot-covered key in his hand. He waited patiently for the sound of small anxious feet to sound down the stone hall.

Some time later the young boy, Thomas, appeared at the cold bars of Harbin's cell with a small bag in his hands. "Sir, I've brought the items you requested!" The boy's voice was full of enthusiasm, yet still only a whisper.

"Good," Harbin responded as he reached out to take the items from the boy. "I heard some noise earlier. Do you know what that is about?"

"Thomas looked worried for a moment and spoke, "The Lord has imprisoned everyone in the keep! They are all being kept in the main cells down the hall.

Is that really part of his plan?" Harbin thought to himself before continuing. "Thank you for telling me. Now, I will attempt to do something quite dangerous. I think this entire coming night will be quite dangerous as well. So, I advise you to gather up some food and a dagger of your own and hide somewhere you won't be found within the keep that is completely dark."

"S-sir, you frighten me with your words. W-will you be alright?" Thomas responded, anxiety in his voice, yet also a strange bit of worry for someone other than himself could be found within it as well.

"I am not sure, young man, but I hope so," Harbin said with a stoic expression on his face. "Now go." With those last words, Thomas clenched his fist once more and ran out of the hall.

With the boy on his way to safety, Harbin pulled out the items from the small bag. First was a smaller bag filled with soot. He took out the dagger and carefully covered it without removing it from the bag in a layer of black powder. After that he carefully tied the blade around his wrist with a bit of thread he had pulled from his clothing. He then pulled out a handful of ash from the other smaller bag and held it carefully in a clenched palm as he used the other hand to pull out a small silver hand mirror.

Careful not to let the mirror be illuminated just yet, he watched as the sun set just a bit more before carefully feeling the amount of ash in his hand. He started to allow a small stream of the powder to fall from his clenched hand, and then, with resolve, he closed his eyes while moving the mirror in front of his face.

"I wish to speak with you, fiend." Harbin wasn't quite sure this would work. After all, it was possible that this dangerous man could be in any reflective surface within the entire keep so he wouldn't need to appear here. However, Harbin had concluded a few things, the first being that whoever this fiend was, could not outright kill someone. He must use another person to harm someone, as could be found from himself being used to strike Mr. Mor. The second was that there was a time limit on his possession, only allowing him to take over someone's body for a few minutes at most. The third was that this fiend wasn't as powerful and omnipresent as he seemed to be, after all, if he was, why was it that when he possessed someone, they always seemed to have their eyes looking at a mirror, or other reflective surface? Why not just do it at his own whim? However, there were still a few questions that remained.

A light and cold laughter filled the dimly lit room. "I am surprised you have figured out my capabilities to this extent, little scribe...." This time, the voice was as cold and calm as ever; however, it didn't hold the same tone and power as it had before. Instead, it resembled Harbin's own voice. This confirmed another thing for Harbin: there weren't two Wyllrans in the room the other night. It was simply the Lord himself and his reflection.

"There is something I wish to know, Mr...?" Harbin spoke once more, trying to prod for the fiend's name.

Light laughter sounded through the chamber once more before the cold yet familiar voice rang out, "I have already made that mistake once, why would I do it again?"

"Then I wish to simply ask you a few questions then." Harbin responded; he knew it was unlikely the fiend would share his name just like that, however, that was simply to 'break the ice' so to speak. "What is your goal with Lord Wyllran, and why have I been dragged into this plot?"

"My goal? Ah, it's not something that I can just share with anyone; however, I will tell you that it involves me getting close with the more powerful members of the Yklan family...." The voice's calculating personality could be heard as clear as day from his words.

"Then why go after Lord Wyllran? Why not his brother, staying upstairs at this very moment?" Harbin prodded.

"Perhaps Wyllran would discuss that with you? Apparently he's already told you so much..." Something else began to creep into the voice's tone.

"Then at least tell me what part I play in this plan of yours," Harbin responded, still calm in his movements.

"You were a loose end...On the off chance I failed here, I could still kill Wyllran before he managed to spill anything, you, on the other hand." Harbin could practically feel the vision of his reflection boring into his own closed eyes. "You have written down many things during your short time in the keep, most of it being dull documents, however… I know you've written down a few things that could be pieced together by a clever mind should they manage to get their hands on it. If you managed to escape with these things, I'd have to fully reconstruct my plans, and that seems like too much of a hassle. At the same time, if I had killed you then, it would have brought panic to the entire keep. Alerting the more important factions at work…"

Harbin went silent for a moment as he felt the amount of ash in his clenched hand dwindling. "So, with what I know now, you will surely wish to kill me; however, you yourself said the keep will go into panic if you do so. What do you plan to do?"

"You forget something, young scribe… Sure, if I had done it that first day or even this day, it would have caused panic. However, you are now seen as a violent drunkard…the moment 'you' make another violent move, I will kill you." The cold voice responded. Harbin could somehow feel the smile on the reflection's face.

"So that's your clever plan? To possess me and make me strike another unknowing victim to your plot?" Harbin calmly replied as he felt the amount of ash in his hand growing smaller and smaller.

"Of course! Isn't it brilliant? Once you are out of the equation, I can fully focus on Wyllran, and once I have him completely, I can burn all those notes you wrote. Completely erasing any trace that I was here." The voice was growing more…deranged as this conversation went on. As if the mere thought of his plan going perfectly was like a high-end drug.

"What about those you have left in your trail? Those with little gaps in their memory? Seems like a miscalculation on your part…" Harbin was growing nervous; provoking this fiend wasn't the smartest thing to do, but he knew it was necessary.

"You little–!" The voice stopped itself as it suddenly took a deep breath. "You are trying to enrage me for this little plot you have created, young scribe… But I won't allow myself to be swayed by such simple tactics." The voice paused for a moment before speaking once more. "I quite think our little confrontation is over, so why don't you...OPEN YOUR EYES!"

Harbin suddenly felt a firm hand around his throat coming from the other side of the metal bars. The hand was gauntleted, seemingly belonging to one of the guards. The other hand of the guard was not in a gauntlet, and it began reaching for Harbin's eyelids, aiming to pry them open.

"You really aren't as smart as you think you are, are you?" Harbin managed to choke out as a smile crossed his own face.

"What do you mean, boy!?" The voice responded again, still coming from the mirror and filled with rage once more.

"You've neglected an important detail about this situation." Harbin continued.

"And what would that be?" The voice seemed to have a hint of confusion and even panic in it this time.

"Mirrors cannot reflect a person's reflection if there is no light with which to do so." Harbin felt the last bit of ash fall from his hand as his makeshift hourglass had finally run out.

"I'll kill you, BASTA–" The voice was cut off as Harbin opened his eyes in the newly dark room, the light from the sun had finally left the chamber once more.

The hands around his neck and face suddenly went slack for a moment before flying into motion, most likely scrambling to find a match or a bit of tinder to make a light. Before this possessed guard could make enough light for the fiend to travel between bodies, Harbin reached into his sleeve and pulled out the dagger. With a surprisingly fast movement, he plunged his soot-covered blade into his opponent's neck via the small gap between the helm and breastplate, killing the man in just a few moments. Thankfully he hadn't been wearing padding or chain underneath his armor.

Moving quickly, Harbin reached into his pocket and pulled out a soot-covered key, careful not to drop it in the process. He reached through the bars and placed it into the keyhole. With a metallic creak, the door to the cell flung open. Harbin looked around the ground as his eyes finally adjusted to the darkness. There, next to the guard's dead body, he found a small hand crossbow in addition to a small quiver attached to the man's belt with a few bolts within it. Harbin gathered up the crossbow and attached the quiver to his own belt, then, with a resolute stride, he began making his way out of the underground prison.

"I wonder what Lord Wyllran's plan will be..."

End of Part 1

7

———

Approaching Storm

"**M**y Lord, we have received word that an abnormal snowstorm will be arriving upon us sometime in the next two to three days." Mr. Mor spoke as he entered the study.

"Thank you for the warning, Mr. Mor. Begin assessing our stockpile to prepare the keep to be isolated for a few days." Lord Wyllran spoke. His voice was deep and resonant, allowing all those who heard it to instinctively trust the man.

As Mr. Mor, his head butler for the past fifteen years, walked out of the room, Wyllran heaved a quiet sigh. He knew that the situation would be relatively fine considering Mr. Mor was at its head. He was a deeply reliable man, perhaps quick to anger at times, but still very trustworthy.

"And, I will be here dealing with this for the next few days without a re-prieve, it seems, thanks to the storm..." Wyllran thought as a stoic look fell upon his slightly wrinkled features. He looked up from the document he was signing and swept his gaze across those who remained in the room.

The first was a small boy standing on the left side of the closed door across from the desk Wyllran was sitting at. His name was Thomas. He was young, only a mere sixteen years old, yet Mr. Mor had chosen him from among a recent pool of candidates to be the newest employee of the keep. He had medium-length auburn hair with a frail build. Currently, he was fidgeting with bits of his new

27

uniform, clearly unaccustomed to wearing things such as dress shirts, vests, and trousers that fit him. Wyllran wasn't sure why Mr. Mor had chosen this specific boy since he was very clearly anxious in almost all facets of the job, but Mr. Mor was an excellent judge of character. Never once in his time as the head butler had his intuition been wrong, so Wyllran chose to trust him.

The other figure sat at another desk that had been temporarily placed in the room. This man wasn't as young as the other, perhaps in his early twenties. He clearly had much more confidence than Thomas, as even when hunched over a piece of parchment, he seemed comfortable. Not just in this space but also within his work, as even though he had spent hours straight copying documents, he had not made even a single mistake. However, he gave Wyllran an odd feeling. The young man, Harbin, rarely spoke unless it was necessary. Wyllran knew that he prided himself on being knowledgeable, considering his career as a scribe; however, he did not seem to flaunt his intelligence as other men his age would. Mr. Mor had chosen this scribe from the main Yklan estate for this reason, as it was told to him, and once again, he simply had to trust the man's intuition.

"Harbin," Wyllran spoke directly at the confident young man, causing him to look up from his work. "I trust that you will not speak of the incoming storm until I have made a proper announcement. Otherwise, it may cause a small panic amongst those in the keep."

The young man met Wyllran's gaze. "Of course, my Lord." Soon after, he returned to his work. Wyllran took the moment to look at the young Thomas, giving him a look as if to say, "You as well," to which he received a nervous nod.

"I need to increase this boy's courage, or he'll never survive in this world..." Wyllran thought to himself as he let out another quiet sigh.

Later on in the day, Wyllran found himself walking through the main hall of his keep with the entourage of Thomas, Harbin, and a few other servants walking behind him. The images of himself and his beloved horse danced across the floor as they walked, making it appear as if the images were moving as they went forward down the hall. *"I should have her brought inside...She will freeze in the cold."* Wyllran had that thought just as Mr. Mor approached him.

"My Lord, I have looked into our stores, and we shall be fine for the next few days; however, the storm is approaching sooner than the scholars originally thought. We received word an hour ago that it will be arriving tonight. They have even reported that the snow will stop falling only two days after that." He informed Wyllran calmly as he joined the entourage at its forefront.

"So specific, have the scholars recently gained some new technology or magic that allows them to get such details?" Wyllran asked curiously as he held a smaller letter in his pocket. *"How odd, I wonder what happened."*

Mr. Mor walked a bit closer to Wyllran, holding out a small piece of parchment instead of giving a response. *"Hmm, what is this?"* He thought as he eyed the calm face of Mr. Mor before he lowered his gaze to the page.

"Official Report for the Northeast area of Volatia.

To the keep of Wyllran Yklan,

The coming storm will arrive this evening, and snow will fall heavily without reprieve until two nights have passed. Naturally occurring storms are hard to predict, so originally, when we received these measurements, we were suspicious. Upon closer inspection, the storm has been created through magical means and has appeared to be localized around the region of your keep. It extends nearly a week's travel in all directions, and a mountain peak to the north of your keep has been identified as its center point. At this time, we are not certain as to the purpose of this storm, nor have we identified the caster.

–Northern Volatia Scholar's Guild."

Wyllran finished reading the message and looked over at Mr. Mor, meeting the man's eyes. "Was this letter sent via carrier pigeon, or a courier?" He spoke in a slightly different tone than normal, something only Mr. Mor could pick up on.

"It was a courier, My Lord." The old man responded with a slight nod, clearly he caught the tone of his employer.

"Make sure that this courier is given rest and a meal before sending them on their way." Wyllran continued.

"Of course, my Lord." Mr. Mor responded as Wyllran handed him a small letter that had been received a few hours prior.

Wyllran spoke in a quieter voice and told the man, "This arrived via carrier pigeon; it died shortly after it arrived." The letter was slightly crumpled and partially stained on the corner with a deep red coloration. Its hurried and scrawled script read,

" outpost destroyed

do not send aid

danger approaches"

Mr. Mor carefully read the letter before looking back up at Wyllran, matching his quieter tone. "This message arrived before the courier was sent from the guild?"

Wyllran nodded with a stern expression on his face. Soon after, Mr. Mor was heading off to the lower parts of the keep near the stables. Wyllran was only able to convey the true meaning of his instruction to Mr. Mor because the man had been with him for so many years. Others may not have caught it; however, Mr. Mor knew that since this courier arrived an hour ago, they most likely began riding after the outpost was destroyed. In short, whoever they were had arrived at the keep under ill intent, so Wyllran had silently conveyed to Mr. Mor that they were to be escorted out of the keep and then killed once they were out of sight.

"*The coming days will be difficult, I'm sure of it.*" He thought as he clenched his fist within his pocket. "Harbin, you will have the rest of today and tomorrow to yourself. Please get some rest." Wyllran said, his features becoming soft once more. After Harbin had bowed and left, Wyllran turned to the young Thomas. "You will announce that all the people within the keep are to gather in the ballroom in the next hour, after that, go out to the stables and have my steed brought into the keep."

"O-of course, my Lord!" The boy replied before scampering off.

8

Precautions

As the hour approached, Wyllran went back up the keep to his chambers high above. From there, he waited for a moment to allow the crowd gathered in the ballroom below to calm a bit. Soon, he approached a doorway built into the wall in the antechamber of his room. Upon opening it, he found himself standing on a balcony high above the gorgeous ballroom floor. He waited another moment as various servants ran throughout the room, making sure candles were lit. Seeing the people gathered below, he finally took a breath and spoke loudly.

"Attention!" The anxious crowd grew silent quickly. "As some of you may already know, a large snowstorm is swiftly approaching."

The crowd whispered among themselves for a moment, and some relieved sighs ran throughout the room as their worry for danger swiftly turned to curiosity at their Lord's next words.

"Our dedicated scholars have predicted that the incoming storm will likely trap us within the keep itself for the next 2 days..." Wyllran paused for a moment to let the words reach the ears of his people. "We have enough within our stores to keep everyone fed and relatively comfortable, so you do not have to worry about such things during this time period."

The people gathered seemed to grow a little excited, especially the non-residents, since normally they would only work within the keep during the day and return to their own homes in the evening. Opportunities to eat food fit for nobility was a rare occasion for these people.

"However, you will all be expected to fulfill your duties as you normally do to the best of your ability. Our keep may become our prison for a small while; however, it does not need to look like one."

That last remark received a small chuckle from the assembled crowd, especially from the nobility seated within a section of the ballroom all their own. Wyllran spared a glance at them, knowing that they would be doing no work of their own.

"Those of you who do not have rooms will be given a small cushion and a blanket from our Head Butler, Mr. Leidan Mor, and then assigned a space here within this very ballroom," Wyllran spoke with a well-practiced authority he had learned from the very man he was mentioning.

"Dinner will be prepared within the kitchen starting in one hour, eight o'clock, and soon after, you will all be asked to remain in either your rooms or within your assigned sleeping space." Wyllran continued. He knew that this order would be seen as odd by some people; however, due to the danger he had been warned of, he didn't want anyone wandering the halls at night. As he said these last few words, he caught the eye of young Harbin down in the crowd. The boy was writing in a large tome, presumably copying down his announcement. He caught the boy's gaze and gave him a slight nod. Wyllran hoped to convey to the boy that his commitment to his duty was admirable. However, he knew in his heart that Harbin was most likely still considering his last statement.

It was quickly approaching evening, and Wyllran had chosen to retire to his chambers early this night. He removed his day clothes and put on a simple linen shirt and a pair of soft trousers to sleep in; however, before he retired fully, he approached his window that faced north. He looked out into the distance and appreciated the silent beauty of the tall mountain range, only a day's ride in the distance. A golden, radiant light bathed its left side, leaving the other drenched in shadow as the sun set. His gaze then lowered until a few small figures came into view. They were barely visible past a small hill; only because his chambers were at the very top of this keep could he see them. Anyone else would need to be at his height to share the same view. From there, he watched as two armored figures on horseback flanked another rider. It was too far away to tell; however, Wyllran knew that this rider would be wearing simplistic leather armor and a traveler's cloak, the outfit perfectly suited to the courier's tasks. As the three figures began descending another hill, they were now truly out of sight. A few minutes later, two armored figures began riding back to the keep, but the courier was nowhere to be seen.

Letting out a truly heavy sigh, Wyllran finally approached his large bed at the back of the room. He laid down but did not cover himself with the various finely crafted blankets. This night, he decided the light and warmth of the fire burning on the right side of the room would be enough. He reached for a glass of liquor on his bedside table and took a small sip before setting the half-full glass back down. He began to close his eyes, and before he knew it, he fell into a deep slumber.

9

The First Encounter

"How does it make you feel?" A strange, cold voice found its way into his ears, awakening him from his slumber.

"What? Has someone broken into my chambers?" Wyllran thought as he gripped the handle of the dagger hidden beneath his pillow.

"What do you mean, stranger?" Wyllran responded. His voice not even showing an ounce of fear as he began to sit up in his bed, letting his hand stay concealed underneath his pillow.

"Killing." The voice responded. Its similarity to his own was uncanny, almost identical. Yet it was much colder, much more sinister.

"Whatever do you mean?" He spoke once more, carefully scanning the room for the individual. He did not see anyone in front of him, so he glanced at the mirror on the wall, scanning its reflection to view the space behind him.

"Don't play dumb, Lord Wyllran..." The voice called as Wyllran realized something truly strange. There didn't appear to be anyone behind him as he looked into the mirror, yet he did see the voice's source. His own reflection began speaking to him from within the silver mirror on his wall. "That poor innocent courier that you killed without ever meeting them."

"It was a precaution since they seemed to have come from a place that had been absolutely destroyed..." Wyllran carefully spoke, assessing the situation. "I assume you had a hand in that?"

"Multiple, however, I assure you that the young man you had slaughtered was nothing more than my transportation. I let him live for that purpose, and as thanks, I would have let him leave. If only to return to find his home burned to the ground." The reflection laughed a bit as he said the last part.

"May I ask why you decided to do such a thing?" Wyllran fully got out of bed, seeing how his opponent was his own reflection, he had reasoned that a knife wouldn't do much good.

"I had to stop word of that storm from getting out, especially to your father. You needn't worry about them, though; I hear death can actually be quite peaceful." The reflection stopped pretending to follow his movements and fully stood up and approached the mirror's surface as if it were no more than a window. "It simply would have gotten in the way of my plans."

"And, what sort of plans are those?" Wyllran began carefully thinking about all the enemies his family had. All of them were mostly due to land disputes and debt, and none that he remembered involved someone capable of magic. He knew that his family was technically related to the main house of Atwood, who ruled Uraum to the south, however their main enemy had died a long time ago. Besides that, there were no powerful magic capable enemies he could think of. "I'm afraid I've been terribly rude; I have not even learned your name, dear stranger."

The voice did not speak for a moment before the cold voice suddenly sounded once more. "I suppose I could tell you since you will be helping me accomplish my plans very, very soon..." The reflection backed up from the mirror's surface and bowed before speaking once more. "I am Meditatio. It is a pleasure to meet you, your Lordship.

"I do not recognize this name; perhaps they are a new enemy my father has acquired; however, it's also possible that our family is a mere stepping stone for whoever this is." Wyllran stood and walked up to the mirror, refusing to show signs of fear. "You have said that I shall be joining

in on your plan very soon. I am interested to hear how that will come about."

The cold voice suddenly laughed, "You have misheard me, Lord Wyllran. I did not say you would be joining me. Merely that you would be helping me."

"I'm afraid I do not see how they are different, Meditatio," Wyllran responded. Something about the voice's tone seemed as though this person was preparing to make a move soon, and so he began to prepare himself as well.

"It is difficult to explain to less intelligent beings…how about I just show you?" The reflection suddenly disappeared.

Wyllran spun around the room, taking in the environment. *"Perhaps they have appeared within the chamber physically."* He looked at his bed; his knife still lay under his pillow. He made a move to lunge forward for the weapon when he suddenly caught sight of his glass of brown liquor, a figure appeared within the firelight reflected on its surface, and Wyllran was no longer in the room.

His senses were off in some way that he could not tell. His vision seemed to be lacking as all he could make out in the new space was a void filled with streams of slowly whirling mist. He could not hear anything within the new space, nor could he feel the ground beneath his feet.

"Where the hell am I?" He thought, panicked as he suddenly caught sight of an orange glow coming from somewhere nearby. Quickly, he began to drift in that direction. As he began to approach, he discovered shapes coming into view around him. At first, he couldn't quite tell what they were. Then he began to see them; the sight filled him with a dread he had never truly experienced before. All around him, floating upright were limp bodies, unmoving. Some were at different heights than others, yet they were all around, only a few feet apart. It was as if he had suddenly been transported to some sort of mass underwater grave.

"Do you like the view?" A familiar voice emerged from the darkness. Its cold and calculating tone had not changed; however, its general sound became a lot more androgynous. It was nearly impossible to tell what kind of person it truly came from.

"Where...am I?" Wyllran called out into the darkness as he bumped into a lifeless body. It appeared to be an older woman in scholarly robes, her face frozen in an emotionless expression. "You can think of it as my wardrobe." The voice responded.

If Wyllran could see its source, he was sure that it had a wicked grin upon its face. "You see, I am somewhat of a master of disguises due to some magic I have created."

"Why have you put me in this wardrobe?" Wyllran had begun to calm himself and continued to drift toward the source of light. He continued to push through lifeless bodies. Some were men, some were women, some were old, and others were young. All kinds of people were gathered in this place, some weren't even people Wyllran noticed as he drifted past a group of small creatures like rabbits and mice.

"You see, Lord Wyllran," The voice responded, appearing to ignore the question. "A disguise at this level works very well in populated areas like cities or castles; however, in smaller areas such as...oh I don't know, a keep? There is a possibility that someone could see me in my disguise, and then happen to run into the real person soon after. This can cause problems, so I came up with a solution. Do you know what that is?"

"I do not," Wyllran responded as he finally began to approach the source of orange light.

He drifted past a group of people dressed in servants' clothing when he finally saw it... A large pair of window-like holes in the void-like space. They were in a very familiar shape...the shape of eyes. Within the eyes, he saw the familiar sight of the fireplace within his bedchambers.

The voice replied, its voice chilling.

"The solution is to simply wear the body of the person you wish to become; this type of disguise is more perfect than anything else."

Wyllran looked back at the ocean of floating bodies. He had referred to them in his own mind as bodies simply because that was the easiest term he could think of, however he had believed them to be arcane constructions up until this point. Now he truly realised that they were actually bodies. They weren't quite dead, but not alive either. It's like their consciousness had been removed, leaving only husks that could be worn by whatever this creature Meditatio truly was.

It was then that Wyllran finally felt it. He felt...sluggish. He felt as though his movements were growing slower and slower, and even his thoughts were becoming hard to maintain. *"This...is...bad..."*

"Temporarily taking over a body is quite simple. I can suppress their consciousness for a little while and simply control it like a puppet; however, true possession is much more difficult..." The voice was becoming hard to understand as Wyllran's thoughts slowed even more. "A full takeover requires me to completely eliminate any other influence within the body's mind. As I'm sure you would have figured out in a few minutes, unfortunately, you will not have that luxury."

Wyllran knew due to the warning from earlier in the day that he needed to be on his guard; even then, he allowed himself to sleep. If Meditatio had attempted this on him during his slumber, Wyllran knew that he would have fallen just like the thousands of others in this space; however, Wyllran knew something he did not. "I assume you did not... know this when you began your plan Meditatio, but my family... is famous in some circles for something... my grandfather blessed us with."

"Hmm? And, what would that be?" The voice seemed to be entertained by whatever this last desperate attempt was.

"We have been blessed; our minds are... much stronger than the average person." Wyllran used the last of his energy to pull himself toward the large pair of eyes.

"What?" The cold voice sounded a little panicked.

Wyllran outstretched his arm and grabbed onto the eye. It was like a window with no glass, allowing him to grab onto the "frame".

"What are you doing!? No!" The voice called out as the thousands of bodies around the void began to stir. No features on their faces moved, yet their bodies lunged at the lone Lord.

Wyllran realized after the explanation from Meditatio that the space he was within right now was contained in his own mind as he and Meditatio currently shared a physical form. If he could get his body through these large eyes, he would be able to force Meditato out of it.

The bodies were now flying toward him with extreme speed. Wyllran grabbed onto the eye with his other hand and began to pull himself through before he felt a hand grab onto his ankle. He looked down and saw an elderly man dressed in royal blue robes. Then another hand grabbed onto him, this time onto his shoulder. This hand belonged to a teenage boy, perhaps a farmer's son. He felt something wrap around his midsection and found the black tentacles of some sort of aquatic creature trying to pull him back into the darkness.

Wyllran screamed as more and more bodies piled onto him, and his muscles ached with the effort as he still slowly managed to pull himself through the eye. As more of his body began to reach through to the other side, the appendages grabbing onto him turned to glowing light as they traveled past this invisible barrier. Leaving the various bodies with less and less to grab onto, he was accelerating his progress. He felt as his consciousness was speeding up, and he also felt as it began to merge with his body once again.

"AHHHHAAH, GET OUT OF—" His voice was cut off as he felt himself partially regain control of his body. He stumbled from his bedroom and found himself out in the main room of his chambers. He felt the presence fully leave his body as tired words fell from his lips. "-my head...."

10

Forced Isolation

The cold voice broke the silence in the room from a mirror hanging on the wall near where Wyllran now found himself standing. "...This is certainly a surprise..."

"Does this mean your plan falls apart now? Knowing that my family cannot be possessed?" Wyllran said to the fiend who had once again taken over his own reflection.

"Not quite," Meditatio responded, his voice filled with a calm malice. "It is still possible. I will just wait until you have fallen asleep...or at least when you won't be expecting me. After all, I can be anyone, as you've seen."

The muffled voice of Mr. Mor could be heard on the other side of the door. It seems as though his scream has alerted his trusted butler and several others.

"I won't sleep then," Wyllran responded, matching his tone. "I will remain aware at all times. I will wait until this storm has passed, and I will ride personally to my family to warn them that you have plans involving us. I will inform all those within this keep to watch others carefully and report to me if they find any strange behavior. You will not succeed."

Meditatio paused for a moment before responding. "If you try to warn anyone of me or anything you have discovered about me, in any way...I will kill them. I would rather kill everyone in this keep than allow you to stop me from progressing my plans. Even if only you are left, I can still manage to spin together some sort of lie to make it all make sense. And I will take you over, even if I have to choke you into slumber with the hands of dear Mr. Mor myself."

"You fiend!" Wyllran responded, his voice agitated yet still quiet. "You will not take me this night! Nor any night for that matter!"

"I will, you wretch," Meditatio responded. "I am that which haunts your mind, Lord Wyllran." The cold voice continued, "That mind of yours…how much more of me can it handle? Before…It…Breaks?"

Wyllran's mind was filled with visions of that ocean of lifeless bodies as they wrapped around him, dragging him into the depths of that void.

*creeeeaaaak

The servant's entrance? Wyllran spun around to see young Harbin holding a firepoker and wobbling around like a drunkard deep into his cups. For a moment, he thought the fiend had already begun attempting to attack him. Fear showed upon his face, and confusion showed on the boy's.

"Lord Wyllran.. Who were you—?" Harbin's question was cut short as a loud bang erupted from the room to the pair's right.

"Search the room!" The familiar voice of Mr. Mor roared into the room. "My Lord, are you alright!?" He continued as he caught sight of Wyllran.

Wyllran still wasn't sure whether or not this was an attack from Meditatio, and as a reflex, he glanced at the mirror to see if the fiend was hiding in his reflection. To his horror, he really was there. His own reflection gave him a slight smirk before Wyllran suddenly found himself standing behind Mr. Mor and a few guards as two of their number were hauling away a confused-looking Harbin. The boy wrestled his head around back toward the open doorway and looked within, meeting the gaze of Wyllran.

All those gathered were staring at Harbin as he was being escorted out, the only person at the back of the crowd being Wyllran himself, who met his gaze with a deep sadness and guilt. He knew that Meditatio must have taken over his body just now in a temporary capacity. Though he had no knowledge of what happened, he guessed that when he took over, he somehow made Harbin out to be some sort of attacker, and he was now being sent down to the prison.

"I am sorry, young Harbin. You should have noticed something going on that isn't normal by now." Wyllran thought to himself before the guards and Mr. Mor left the room.

Now left all alone in his chambers once more, Wyllran approached the fireplace. Its flame was dying; however, instead of adding more logs, he let it die. Then, gathering soot from around the bricks surrounding the fireplace, he navigated to every reflective surface in his chambers that he could find. In complete darkness, he rubbed the blackened powder onto them in layers, not allowing anything to give his enemy a doorway within.

Wyllran then, with cautious movements, struck a match within his hands. He quickly looked around, not seeing any light beaming back at him. He moved to relight the fire and fill the space with warmth once more.

11

Pieces of the Puzzle

Shortly after he lit the fire, Wyllran was already preparing his next move. He knew in his heart that Harbin was smart enough to realize that he was framed by someone, and that this person was using methods beyond the realm of the mundane. What they really needed, however, was a way to defeat this person, or trap him at least. For this to work, however, Wyllran himself needed to come up with a method, and to do that, he needed to read.

Beside his bed was a rope connecting through the keep all the way to Mr. Mor's office a few floors below. No more than fifteen minutes after ringing the bell, young Thomas arrived at the door, ready to receive orders from Wyllran and give them to Mr. Mor.

"W-what can I help you with, my Lord?" The boy spoke with even more anxiety than the last time Wyllran saw him.

"How is he even more anxious?" He thought to himself before responding. "Thomas, can you read?"

"I-I can, my lord."

"Good." Wyllran was a bit surprised that the boy could read, considering he didn't receive much education, however Mr. Mor wouldn't pick someone incapable. "I need you to gather these tomes from my study."

Wyllran handed the boy a small note with a list of books before sending him off.

A short time later, he arrived back at the door with what he requested. "Thank you, Thomas."

"O-of course, my Lord." The boy responded, clearly still anxious.

Wyllran bid the boy farewell and returned to his bedchambers. Getting into bed, he placed all the books in front of him. Some titles referred to the use and general knowledge of the arcane, some concerning the supernatural, and some containing general knowledge of physics relating to light and mirrors.

Over the next several hours, Wyllran poured over the books. Every time that he found himself growing tired, he would reach underneath his pillow and press the point of his dagger into his arm, allowing the pain to keep him alert. After laying out a few facts within his mind, he began to formulate a plan. It would be difficult to pull off, yet he believed it might work.

"And this is the first step." He thought to himself as he extinguished his candlelight and pulled a ring of iron keys from his bedside cabinet. Feeling them carefully in the darkness, he located the one he was looking for, the master key for the cells far below. Freeing it from the ring in which they were kept, he placed the rest back in the cabinet and took out his knife. He began scratching and mangling the large key as best he could before relighting his candle, then the larger fire in the room. With a pair of large tongs used to move logs within the fire, he instead held the key over the orange flame. He hoped that the key would heat up enough for him to mangle the handle just a bit more, just enough so that it was no longer reflective in a meaningful way. Next, he went out into the main chamber to the extinguished fire from earlier on in the night, there he again collected soot and rubbed it onto the rather untouched main part of the key. He had made sure the handle was destroyed enough to not be reflective, but he could not do the same with the tip, for fear of making it useless, so he had to make do with the soot.

He then approached his closet to put on a set of comfortable clothing and removed any unnecessary buttons or buckles, rubbing soot upon the rest. He then took a candle and began to make his way down to the cells far below.

Wyllran eventually found his way to the bottom floor of the keep. It's cold stone devoid of any meaningful light was usually a cause of discomfort, however Wyllran could only find sanctuary in the darkness due to the recent events. Passing through the larger holding space Wyllran turned down a smaller hall and found himself in front of a more solitary cell.

"Stay quiet, young Harbin," Wyllran spoke with suspicion in his voice as he swept his gaze across the room. "I do not see him nearby; however, I still can't be too careful." He quickly put out the candle he was carrying in his hand, plunging the room into pitch darkness.

"Why have you done this to me, Lord Wyllran? Or was it this "him" you speak of?" Harbin responded, nearly silent with his questions.

Wyllran heaved a quiet sigh knowing that Harbin had already begun to consider his true dilemma. Unrelaxing his muscles for a moment, Wyllran felt the exhaustion creep up on him before quelling it once more.

"I cannot tell you specifics, even these words now are at the risk of your life," Wyllran spoke as he bent down a little and got closer to the bars. "You were framed, you know who has done it." After those words, Wyllran dropped the cloth-wrapped key onto the cell's floor.

"Open it after I have left and prepare for tomorrow night. I have a plan, meet me in the ballroom." Wyllran then took out a match and relit the candle in his hand before quickly moving out of the prison corridor and up into the main keep.

12

Plan in Motion

As the sun rose on the second day of the storm, Wyllran had begun the larger preparations of his plan. It was difficult to do something on such a scale without letting anyone in on it. Even if he wished to ask someone for their help, he would only be able to give vague or very short instructions to not reveal the whole plot, since Meditatio could be hiding anywhere.

The first step had already been taken, giving Harbin the key, however many more steps needed to follow to accomplish his goals. The next one is to prepare for Meditatio's immediate attacks. From a logical standpoint, Meditatio will target the guards for his possession. Considering that most are wearing at least half-plate, they are considerably reflective in addition to being trained as fighters; their bodies are much heartier and prepared to kill than someone like the young Thomas. Therefore, Meditatio is likely in the barracks right now, slowly but surely taking over as many of them as he can. He will also realize that the best way to utilize those soldiers is in a large space such as the ballroom. Wyllran has also realized this, of course, and so naturally he will try to thin out their numbers long before they arrive there.

"But first, I need to get the rest of the people somewhere safe." Wyllan let out a sigh, knowing that many will call him mad for what he is about to do next. He once again reached to his bedside and pulled the rope, sending a signal to Mr. Mor.

A few moments later, Mr. Mor himself was at his door.

"Mr. Mor? I admit I was going to ask to see you specifically; however, I expected to talk with young Thomas first." Wyllran spoke, a bit surprised.

"Yes, my Lord. Thomas has apparently disappeared for the moment. I saw him earlier in the day, however it appears as though he has not been around since."

"I hope the poor boy has not been taken by Meditatio..." Wyllran thought to himself, more than a bit worried for the anxious young lad. "Well then, I suppose I shall continue on with my orders."

"Please do, my Lord." Mr. Mor spoke as he bowed his head slightly.

"Please make sure that everyone in the keep who has their own chambers is locked within them. After that, please go down to the ballroom and have the kitchen staff feed all those present. Following that, escort them all, including servants, down to the dungeons and imprison them."

Silence fell over the space.

"Surely you jest, my Lord?" Mr. Mor looked quite concerned.

"I do not, Mr. Mor. Please begin your work." Wyllran responded. "Oh, and Mr. Mor?"

Mr. Mor turned around moments after he began to leave. "Please imprison yourself along with them."

"A-as you wish, my Lord..." The old butler seemed very concerned about the whole situation, but he knew deep in his heart that Wyllran knew what he was doing.

After a while, the sounds of indignant shouts and confusion rolled through the keep, signalling that the plan was truly in motion. Wyllran looked at the sunlight trying to creep in through the soot-covered window as he began considering his next course of action.

"Now that the stage is set, I must do the next step alone."

Without the help of servants or other staff to aid him, Wyllran began the next task alone. Carefully, he went down to the ballroom. He chose to enter into the servants' passageways because they were less prone to having reflective surfaces and were rather dark even during the day.

Some time later, he found himself standing in front of an extremely large fireplace built into the wall of the opulent ballroom. There was no light except for the candle in his hands, yet Wyllran was still on his guard for the fiendish reflection. To his surprise, it did not show its face. Yet that didn't mean he wasn't in the room.

"I doubt he's here." Wyllran thought to himself. During his studies the previous night, he had concluded a couple of things about Meditatio's power. The first being that when he is hiding within a reflection, he is bound to it. Meaning that he cannot leave that reflection until another living creature is present for him to move through via possession or simply hiding within their eyes. This is what he discovered after a bit of thought on the fiend calling that courier his "transportation", after all, if he could just appear anywhere he wished, why would he need transportation? The other thing he discovered is that while Meditatio himself has admitted to having only a temporary control over people when possessing them superficially, something Wyllran concluded while looking at books on magic is that he could possess many people at once if they were all under total control. He was able to do it with the 'bodies' of people within his mindscape, and theoretically, if he were able to completely take over many people in the real world, there is a possibility he would be able to do the same.

Since Meditatio is most likely gathering forces within the barracks, it's unlikely he would be traveling around the keep via reflective surfaces. And even if he was, his easiest way of doing so would be through the eyes, buttons, glasses, jewelry, etc., of all the people that would normally be moving around the keep; however, due to Wyllran's order, they were all tucked away in the cells beneath the keep.

Wyllran tightened his grip on the brush he had brought along with him and began to sweep the large fireplace in front of him, gathering as much soot as he possibly could.

Over the course of the next several hours, Wyllran walked along a specific route within his halls with only a single candle to light his way. Carefully, he made sure to rub soot along every silver sconce, every opulent painting's frame, every doorhandle, every window, and every latch. He even managed to track enough soot along the floor that his candlelight no longer reflected upon the marvelous marble, although the depiction upon them could still be seen.

Finally, Wyllran ended up in a specific room. A small and nearly empty room, its only decoration being a tall floor-length mirror with a large cloth piled on top of it, however, not obscuring its reflective surface.

After that, Wyllran made his way back to a large room near the exit into the stables. There, he found his precious mount. A regal chestnut colored warhorse with its black mane braided into small knots evenly placed down its neck.

The horse huffed out a breath as it saw its master approaching. It lowered its head over the makeshift stall that had been set up. Wyllran placed his hand on the horse's neck, feeling its powerful breath. "You know it, don't you?"

The horse gave no apparent response, Wyllran continued anyway. "A battle is coming, and I am not sure if I will survive it."

The horse moved its head down onto Wyllran's shoulder, seemingly acknowledging his feelings. It too seemed ready for battle.

Wyllran began the process of getting his horse ready to ride. He looked out to a nearby soot-covered window, and as the glow from the outside sun began to dim, he knew that the battle was imminent. After getting his horse saddled, he put out his candlelight, and in complete darkness, he began affixing a few pieces of armor to it, covering it in soot as he went along.

With a sigh, he looked off into the keep as darkness fell. The orange glow of the torches he had lit inside beckoned him to enter. After affixing a few pieces of soot-covered armor and a sword to himself, he mounted his horse and spoke. "Time to begin."

End of Part 2

13

Puppets

Harbin began to run down the hall from his isolated cell at the back of the prison beneath the keep. His boots created an echo in the small stone passageway until the sound was muffled by many yelling voices.

"How could he do this!? I won't stand for this treatment! We didn't do anything wrong! Why won't they tell us anything!?" The voices clamoured as their sources came into view. Harbin halted for a moment as he stared at the sight. To either side of him were walls lined with cells, each one packed to the brim with servants, guests, merchants, and cooks.

"*Wow...this is...*" Harbin had been told by Thomas that Lord Wyllran had imprisoned all of these people without even a reason, but to truly see it in person. It stunned him to say the least. However, his encounter just a few moments ago with that fiend had tempered his emotions to the point of being able to simply walk away from this place. And that is what he did.

"You're that scribe! Why are you free!? He's got a key! Let us out! Free us! We didn't do anything!" Harbin ignored the voices and swiftly walked past them, clutching his new crossbow as he prepared for what was ahead.

Truth be told, he really had no idea of what was about to happen. Lord Wyllran had told him that he had a plan and that he should join him in the ballroom, but beyond that, he had no idea.

Quickly, he made his way up the spiraling stone steps to the keep's second floor above. As he began to approach the final steps, he heard what sounded like heavy footfalls heading his way. He pressed himself to the wall, just barely out of the torchlight, and leveled his crossbow.

As the footsteps grew louder, Harbin could begin to make out their numbers. It sounded as if only two figures were approaching, and that fact was soon confirmed as their shadows appeared along the wall. One held a torch and shield, while the other held only a spear. Harbin cautiously inched closer to the doorway to make out the actual forms of his presumed attackers. The torchbearer wore a simple chain shirt with no other adornments other than regular clothing. The spearman had an iron breastplate, bracers, grieves, and a helm; he strangely wore no chain or padding beneath it. It was as if these soldiers did not know how to properly put on their armor, even though they had been trained to do so. Seeing this strange detail, Harbin looked closer. Bathed in the dim orange glow of their torchlight, he could make out their features; both had completely emotionless faces. It was as if they were no more than wooden dolls pulled about on marionette strings, although much more articulated.

Harbin knew that it would take him no less than thirty seconds to reload his crossbow, meaning it was unlikely he would get off more than two shots. So, he had to play this smart. He crouched carefully as the pair began to walk a little past the open stone doorway. Aiming his crossbow, he placed his sight on the arm of the torchbearer. Eliminating the light would be the best course of action since he was at such a disadvantage. As the two entered into the perfect spot, Harbin exhaled a silent breath and fired.

The bolt flew through the air and plunged straight into the wrist of the unsuspecting torchbearer. As blood began to spill on the ground, the torch fell from his grasp and hit the ground before rolling some distance away. The spearman emotionlessly searched for where the bolt emerged as Harbin frantically reloaded his crossbow. The former torchbearer looked down at their wrist and reached across with their other hand, allowing only the straps on their forearm to hold the shield in place. They grasped the bolt with a firm hand and pulled it out in one flawless motion. It never even made a sound as fear and pain meant nothing to this possessed creature.

click The sound seemed thunderous in the quiet hall as Harbin finally managed to load another bolt in the crossbow, aiming it once more. The noise seemed to have caught the attention of the spearman, prompting him to charge in Harbin's direction with his spear leveled. Carefully placing the sights along the man's throat, with a slight pull from his fingers, the bolt flew. The strike caused the man to shudder for a moment as blood began to pool in his throat. His body began to convulse as he choked; only the most bodily sounds emerged from the man, and this one, too, did not fear death or pain. Silently and emotionlessly, it died, dropping the spear from its firm grasp.

Harbin lunged for the weapon as the point of a kite shield was thrust into the space where his head had been just moments before. It seemed as though the former torchbearer had caught up. Rolling to the side to avoid another strike as the kite shield plunged downward into the stone floor, Harbin soon managed to get back up, now wielding the iron-tipped spear. He hefted the long polearm over his knee and snapped it in half; such a long weapon would not be a good fit against the shield. Now with only about a three-foot-long handle with an iron spike at the end, Harbin charged forward, nearly as silent as his opponent as he became immensely focused.

The newly appointed shieldbearer threw a heavy punch toward Harbin. He knew just one solid hit from this creature, and he would be down. However, he was much faster than his enemy. He held his half spear in his right hand and grabbed onto the shield with his left, pulling it down with all the strength he could muster. Then with a swift movement, he plunged the sharp spike down into the shield-bearer's chest, just behind his clavicle and into his heart. With an emotionless plop, the shieldbearer fell to the ground dead.

Harbin quickly removed the shield from the dead soldier, attaching it to his own left arm and holding the half spear in his right. He had decided to abandon the crossbow, since it seemed in the fight ahead, it would be difficult to find time to reload.

With a rather confident stride, Harbin once again began walking to the ballroom.

14

Faithful Steed

As Wyllran rode down the large and opulent halls of his keep, the sound of dozens of armored boots hitting the ground stuck in his ears. It echoed down the halls like the rolling of metallic thunder. He eventually came to face them as the group revealed themselves at the end of a long hall, Wyllran at the other end with his horse facing away toward another direction.

"Meditatio!" He roared, his own voice reverberating in his helm.

One soldier stepped forward, clearly different from those around him. Wyllran recognized his face to be that of Captain Dryn, the leader of his soldiers. The man's features initially appeared to be as emotionless as those surrounding him, however as he lowered a large greatsword, Wyllran caught a good look at his face in the torchlight burning on the wall nearby.

The man stepped forward, and with a cold expression, he bowed mockingly, "My Lord...."

Meditatio stood up from his bow and tried to meet Wyllran's eyes from behind his soot-covered helm. "I was hoping that your mind had been lost after a day of panic due to your stunt earlier today, however... seeing you now makes me think otherwise."

Wyllran held aloft a once magnificent longsword that was now covered in soot. "The only thing I have lost, fiend, is fear for my life. I will not remain hidden in my chambers, going mad over your threats, and instead, I will choose to defeat you. If it costs my life to do so…so be it."

"Perhaps I can reinstill that fear in your mind," Meditatio responded with the gravely voice of the man he possessed. Then he lofted the greatsword aloft with only one hand and pointed down the hall with it. As he did, the swarm of emotionless soldiers brandished their spears, swords, shields, and other weaponry. Only a moment after that, they began to charge after their former Lord.

Wyllran gripped the reins of his horse tightly in his gauntlet, then, with a quick pull, he galloped down the torchlit hall toward the ballroom. He believed he was much faster than his pursuers at first, yet it was only a moment later that he found himself turning to look behind at the swarm. There he saw a strange sight. The soldiers were all independent creatures, yet in this moment, they held no fear and worked in perfect unison under the control of Meditatio. The soldiers sprinted and ran over top of one another, some collapsed under the weight, and others began to be pressed against the walls. They were like a writhing mass of metal-clad maggots on their way to devour a rotting corpse. Wyllran predicted that they would act like this; however, what he didn't expect was that their seemingly self-destructive movement did not thin their numbers nor slow them down. Instead, those who had been trampled and crushed into the walls cracked their joints and bones back into place as best they could, not for any pain they were experiencing but simply to preserve their mobility. As soon as a soldier was trampled, they would serve as a platform for others to cross upon, then, when the crowd began to thin, they would stand and reset their bodies. They would then begin to sprint as best they could and rejoin the main force, and trample others beneath their own feet in a gruesome, violent, and unstoppable cycle.

Meditato ran at the forefront of the group, not allowing his main body to be trampled. He did not yell orders, but instead, with nothing more than a momentary halt that lasted no more than a second, a group of soldiers split off. These ones held crossbows, javelins, and spears. Without even needing to take time and aim due to their perfect control, they launched their projectiles to rain down upon their prey.

Wyllran quickly pulled the reins of his steed and turned down another hall, allowing the majority of the projectiles to pierce into the wall. As the swarm crashed like a wave into the very same obstacle, some were impaled on the various newly formed spikes. Those who were able to, pulled themselves from the wall and left themselves with gaping holes across their bodies. However, if the injury did not stall their movement, it was simply left to be. Blood gushed from their wounds, and soon the endless cycle of the swarm became drenched in crimson.

Quickly turning down another corridor, Wyllran firmly grasped onto the saddle and gave his horse a slight kick as they approached a stairway leading down to the next floor. For what felt like an eternity, Wyllran and his noble steed were suspended in the air as the swarm of blood-soaked soldiers roiled on the staircase beneath them. With a sickening crunch, the horse's hooves landed firmly onto a few unfortunate soldiers near the front, crushing their helms and heads within them in an instant. With another hard pull, Wyllran whipped his steed around and pointed it in the direction of the next hall, only to find it had grown much slower.

The horse shook its head and gave a gut-wrenching whinney as it lifted one of its front legs into the air. "NO!" Wyllran yelled, his own voice echoing in his ear within the helm.

Only a moment later, the heavy greatsword of Meditatio's body cleaved through the horse's neck, severing it halfway.

As tears welled within his eyes, he leaped from his steed as it collapsed at the entrance to the hall. Its final sacrifice provided a barrier to slow the approaching swarm for a few moments, allowing Wyllran to sprint forward on foot. His armored grieves thudding against the marble floor depicting himself upon that very steed were almost impossible to hear as the crunching of metal from behind echoed in the hall.

15

Brave Boy

Harbin heard horrifying sounds beneath him. He could tell that it was an armored force of soldiers, as he had been on the battlefield before in a scribe capacity, but never had he heard a group that large fighting silently. Recalling the emotionless soldiers from a few moments ago, he pieced together that this force was most likely that of the nameless fiend besieging the keep.

He knew that he was only one man with barely any fighting experience at that, so he would have to find a different way down to the ballroom. With quick steps and a quicker mind, he once again found himself entering the servants' passageway. The narrow corridor and low lightning was suddenly very frightening as the thought of a fiendish villain roaming the keep crept into Harbin's mind. He knew enough about combat to realize he wouldn't be able to make good use of the half-spear and shield he had acquired in this space, so he carefully attached the spear to his hip and held the shield in front of him with both hands as he made his way down to the lower floor.

Due to the thick walls between himself and the main keep's corridors, he could no longer quite hear the sounds of battle somewhere below him, and instead, the space became eerily quiet.

The only sound accompanying him was the sounds of flickering candlelight placed every so often in the hall and his own footsteps.

*tap   *tap   *tap   *tap

The sound became almost a rhythmic anchor for Harbin's panicked heart, though he knew better than to relax. He held the shield in front of himself, bracing for the attack he just *knew* was approaching. However, several silent moments passed with nothing happening as he slowly passed by Mr. Mor's office.

*tap   *tap   *tap   *tap   *tap *tap

"What?" Harbin tried to whip his body around as he thought he heard another step behind him…one he did not take. As he tried, his shield prevented him as he caught it on the wall. He quickly began trying to turn to face this incoming attacker as he suddenly felt something hot against his side.

Pausing his efforts, he looked down at his stomach. There, on his right side, was a dagger plunged deep into him. The dagger was quickly pulled from his skin, and a rich crimson color began to darken his clothing. He looked up at his attacker as blood dripped from a longer silver blade.

Standing on the steps above him, meeting his own eyeline was a young boy dressed in a white dress shirt now partially stained with blood spatter, a black vest, and a pair of well-fitted black trousers. Holding the knife was the anxious young boy Thomas, his face expressionless.

"no…" Was all Harbin managed to say before the knife swung in his direction again. Quickly, he dropped the shield and turned to face the boy properly, allowing the knife to miss slashing his back. That's when Harbin noticed something. A clock a few steps above him, near the doorway to Mr. Mor's office, and tears welling in the emotionless eyes of Thomas.

"You're not fully taken, are you?" Harbin said to the boy, and he raised his hands into the air in front of him.

A cold voice responded, seemingly a bit tired. "If you were more of a fool, this would have been much easier."

A hollow laugh escaped from Harbin's lips. "I only have to last a few minutes then.."

The voice responded with a cold bit of laughter of its own. "You may certainly try."

Suddenly, Thomas stopped speaking and lashed out once more, attempting to bring his knife down upon Harbin's chest.

Carefully and expertly minimizing the damage, Harbin held his arm in the blade's path. The knife stabbed straight through his forearm; however, that was much better than his chest. The formerly anxious boy wrenched the knife free and lowered his angle, attempting to stab through Harbim's defence and pierce his ribcage. His now injured arm did not move as fast as the previous attempt, while his other was not in the right position entirely. The blade effortlessly cut through the air; however, just before it managed to break skin, it suddenly slowed and veered off course. The blade sank into his shoulder instead, and Harbin looked up at the boy, surprised.

On the boy's face, he saw the emotionless exp[ression on his lower features like his mouth and cheeks, however his eyes were scrunched tightly with a silent fury as tears fell from them to the ground.

"*He's... fighting back!?*" Harbin only had a moment for such a thought before a yell escaped the mouth of Thomas. "Foolish child! Stop your useless struggle!"

Thomas's face went completely slack for a moment as he raised his right leg and planted it firmly on Harbin's chest. The force wasn't all that great; however, it was enough to send an injured man falling down a flight of stairs.

"No!" The panicked sound escaped his lips as Harbin suddenly felt dizzy. He found himself on a landing about fifteen feet from where he was before. His left arm now bent at an odd angle, and blood trickling down from his scalp as he began to sit up. Through blurred vision, Harbin looked up as the small frame of Thomas was suddenly upon him. The boy was kneeling on his chest, causing what little air Harbin had left in his lungs to escape. Neither words nor shouts of pain could leave his lips as he desperately tried to suck in air.

"This is where it ends, scribe." The youthful voice of Thomas spoke once more in a chilly tone. The emotionless expression remained as both of his hands gripped the handle of the dagger. He raised it above his head, preparing to plunge it right into Harbin's body.

"Maybe it really is where it ends..." Harbin thought what he guessed would be his last remark. However, the blade did not fall. Instead, he looked up at the boy's face as some of his blurred vision began to return to normal. It was just enough for him to view Thomas's face. One eye was completely focused with its vision directly pointed at the blade in his hands. The other eye was filled with tears, and its pupil was dilated.

"I-I...." The voice emerging from the boy was no longer as calm and cold as it had been just moments ago. Instead, it was filled with raw emotion. Some mixture of fear, some anger, and some great will to retake his own body. "...won't.....LET YOU!"

In that moment, there was something absent from that voice. There was not even a shred of anxiety.

The blood-soaked dagger fell swiftly in an arc from above Thomas's head, and instead of striking Harbin's chest. It instead penetrated deeply into the boy's own chest.

"ACK—!" The sound emerged almost of its own accord from Thomas's mouth as blood began spilling out from his lips. In this moment, Harbin knew that the fiend had been banished from this boy's body completely.

"Thomas...." Harbin could barely manage to say his name as the boy collapsed off of his own body, falling hard on the stair's landing next to him.

"Sir Harbin–" Thomas's words were cut off as he coughed up more blood. "Go...Lord Wyllran has a plan...and you must help him..."

"Of course..." Harbin forced himself to sit up and meet the boy's eyes. Not allowing himself to look away as the light slowly faded from them. "You are brave, Thomas."

A smile crept across the features of the boy as a final breath escaped his body.

16

A True Fiend

Wyllran sprinted down the grand hallway, the blood of his steed dripping from his armor and leaving river-like patterns on the soot-covered surface. He could hear the cacophony of the armored swarm behind him. Thanks to his horse, there was now a larger gap between him and Meditatio; however, Wyllran knew that it wouldn't last long. As he ran, he ripped a torch off the wall, holding it aloft in his hands as he approached the final stretch to the grand double doors of the ballroom.

As he progressed, he could feel the reverberations in the ground as the soldiers were now once again hot on his heels. Turning a corner at breakneck speed and simply allowing himself to crash into the wall slightly to avoid slowing down, he could now behold them. Two large doors carved from a deep colored wood with the visage of an armored knight rising out from their surface.

As he beheld the magnificent figure, a familiar smell hit his nostrils. The acrid smell of lantern oil permeated the space. This was something Wyllran had done during his preparations earlier in the day.

His armored boot crashed into the slightly damp floor. Every step he made was as fast as he dared to go; even a single mistake could cause him to slip and drop the torch into the oil. He planned to burn his pursuers, not himself, so there was no space for such a mistake.

The swarm finally emerged into the hall, their roiling form refusing to slow down even as Meditatio's face revealed a sense of recognition from the scent in the air. Instead of halting, he silently commanded his army to slow down, leaving him far in the lead. Knowing the fiend's intelligence, Wyllran guessed that the man knew he was trying to burn the main force during his attack and that he wouldn't light the oil early for fear of messing up the timing.

"Do you think you're clever, Wyllran!?" Meditatio's voice filled the hall as Wyllran suddenly stopped in front of the large doorway.

"No, Meditatio." Wyllran turned to face the approaching force and planted his sword firmly in the stone, standing tall in front of the doors. "I am wise." With that, Wyllran tossed the torch out in front of him down the hall.

The hall suddenly became illuminated in bright orange light as the flames raced across the ground. The immolating heat swallowed Meditatio and the roiling swarm of bloody soldiers behind him. Even as they burned, these emotionless puppets let out no screams of agony or fear.

Wyllran watched silently as the swarm slowly came to a halt. Their armor began to heat up and bend at odd angles as they continued to trample one another. The exposed skin charred and melted, revealing bloody muscle beneath it. And, even though Wyllran could not see it, he knew that the skin under their armor would begin to stick and burn onto the inside of the metal. Entombing them in their own personal coffins. Wyllran watched as their bodies began to die and their movement drastically decreased, and after a moment, he turned back around and placed a hand on either of the double doors. With a heave, he pushed them open to reveal the ballroom in front of him, another doorway open on the other side.

He began taking heavy, tired steps forward when the sound of metal scraping the ground emerged from behind him. Looking backwards, he saw a partially charred body covered in flame and bent armor walking toward him. The skin on its face had partially burned away, leaving only one eye upon its newly revealed blackened skull. The flaming half-corpse dragged a long greatsword behind it as it walked with purpose toward Wyllran. Meditatio was approaching once more.

"I do not feel pain, yet moving this body is growing quite uncomfortable..." Its voice was as cold as ever, only now it was much more strained and seemingly dry.

"I wouldn't want you to be uncomfortable. Perhaps you should just go ahead and die. I've heard that death is actually quite peaceful." Wyllran responded, raising his own sword with two hands as he turned around fully to face the now truly fiendish Meditatio.

17

A Lord's Promise

Harbin was holding his side with his injured hand as he held his half spear in front of him. He was quickly approaching the servant's door to the ballroom when he began to smell smoke and burning flesh. Hurrying his steps, he pressed down on the small metal latch and pushed open the door, revealing the cavernous chamber. In front of him, he found a pair of figures brandishing weapons. The figure with its back turned to him appeared to be Lord Wyllran. His armor was covered in soot and blood as his shoulders sank with fatigue. His longsword was held aloft, pointing at a terrifying creature similarly holding a long greatsword.

The second figure would be better described as a creature that had crawled from the depths of hell. Its blackened skull was exposed as its face had melted halfway, leaving it with very few features with which it could show emotion, however one thing remained. A single cold and calculating eye swiveled within its socket as flames burned across its form. Unfazed by the heat and pain of its own body burning away.

"Lord Wyllran!" Harbin hurried forward, grateful that his legs had not been harmed too badly in his journey to this point.

"Is that you harbin!?" Wyllran shouted back. He didn't dare take his eyes away from the devil in front of him.

"It is my Lord!" He hurriedly responded. "What do you need of me!?" His voice was nearly drowned out by the roar of flames coming from behind the hellish walking corpse.

"Go through the doors behind you! It will lead you to safety!" Wyllran responded as he inched closer to the skeleton.

Harbin hesitated for a moment; he knew that these doors would not lead to an exit from the keep. He also knew that Wyllran would not have given him a key and told him he had a plan if all Harbin needed to do was leave. Harbin looked at the two figures silently for a moment. *"He is trying to deceive that creature. He knows that it will likely follow me to prevent my escape, and he plans to fight it here and stall for time..."*

"Go Harbin! You can find the way out of this mess, I know you can! I will hold him off, I swear it!" Wyllran called out as he finally lunged at the flaming corpse, its own blade connecting with his and throwing it aside, deflecting the blow.

Harbin swallowed hard and dashed down the hall.

...

Wyllran heard the young scribe's footsteps hitting the stone floor behind him, slowly growing more faint.

"This is your plan!?" The corpse let out a haughty growl. "To let yourself die for his escape? Even if he does, the storm will still rage for a few more hours. I'll catch him as soon as I'm done with you!" The greatsword twirled in the air, turning to deflect the longword before being raised up as the corpse's body extended. Allowing the greatsword to fall toward Wyllran's shoulder.

The blow fell heavily upon his pauldron and slid off. The strike nearly made him collapse to his knees as the fatigue was finally creeping up on him. "Even if I die, you will be defeated one way or another." Wyllan breathed in, allowing his body to swell with strength and energy for his final few moments.

He turned his body, allowing his longsword to return in front of him. He sidestepped a lunge from Meditatio and lunged forward himself, letting the tip of his blade crack into the deformed armor upon the walking corpse's body, plunging into its midsection.

"I've seen this too many times to count, you wretch." Meditatio began as he stepped forward, simply allowing his body to be skewered on the longsword. "A desperate last struggle that ends in defeat."

Wyllran did not respond. He attempted to pull his blade free, however Meditatio's charred hand gripped his own, causing him to keep his hands wrapped around the handle. The villain changed his grip on the greatsword, holding it by the blade near the crossguard with the handle pointed upwards. "Even if your death prevents me from following him for even a few extra seconds, it ultimately will not matter!"

Meditatio suddenly ripped himself off the blade as he leaned backwards. Following that, a powerful armored kick landed upon Wyllran's gut. Wyllran refused to fall. Seeing his prey no longer responding, the fiend used his other hand to grab the greatsword halfway down the blade.

Wyllran raised his sword to block the impending strike, however Meditatio's sword fell behind his own, halting its movement as the crossguard hooked under his armpit. Then, with a mighty heave, Meditatio pushed Wyllran to the ground. As his head struck the marble floor, his helmet flew off, exposing his exhausted expression.

"I'll have to find another way to sneak into house Yklan, because–" The blade was placed against Wyllran's throat. "--I really want to kill you."

"The feeling is mutual." Wyllran finally responded as he gripped the sides of the flaming skull.

Then two separate things went into motion at the same time. The sword cut across Wyllran's neck, allowing his crimson blood to stain his armor and spill to the floor. In the same moment, Wyllran willed all the strength he had left to abandon any attempts at survival. Instead, it flowed into his arms and hands, and cracks began to form on the skull before it crumbled into pieces.

18

A Desperate Gamble

The sound of clanging steel filled the dimly lit hall as Harbin hurried through it. He knew in his heart that Wyllran had truly left everything to him. He wasn't sure how to feel knowing that someone had so much faith that he would be able to defeat such a creature; however, he did not have time to think about that right now. What he needed to do was figure out how to make use of the steps Wyllran had laid out for him.

As he ran through the hall, Harbin carefully looked at his surroundings. Nearly everything here was covered in a layer of soot, seemingly to prevent that villain from pursuing; however, spaced evenly from the last were various reflexive objects. Some were blades, others were small hand mirrors, some pieces of glass, etc. It seemed as though it was a path for the mirror fiend to travel through. But where did it lead?

Harbin raced through the hall for nearly a full minute before he heard the sound.

A hauntingly cold voice yelled from somewhere behind him. "Get back here, boy!"

Harbin continued running; however, his curiosity got the best of him, and he cautioned a look behind him. There he saw the visage of himself reflected in the flat of a large ornamental sword. The reflection's only similarity to him was its form. The way it moved, the expression it made, and the chilling laughter escaping from it were nothing short of horrifying.

It flew from reflection to reflection, chasing him like a wraith that only existed within the mirrored world.

"Did you know he died for this plan of yours?!" The voice screamed from behind him. "I slit his throat and watched as the blood stained his precious keep's floor!"

Harbin continued to sprint down the hall, blood from his own injuries dripping onto the soot below as he went, creating more reflective surfaces for him to be followed. Harbin took a moment to look down as a drop of blood fell through the air from his arm. Time seemed to slow for a moment as Harbin saw his own face reflected within it, then it moved. A familiar injured hand reached toward the surface of the reflection as the fiend let out a pained scream.

"AHHH—!" The villain shrieked as he seemingly strained his capabilities to their very limit. Then the drop of blood's surface rippled as it flattened out into a circular thin disc, allowing his reflection's hand to burst from it and grab onto his own. The hand clenched onto the wound in his arm powerfully. Screaming in pain, Harbin managed to shake off the hand as time moved at the right speed once again.

Then, in front of him was a piece of broken glass the size of a dinner plate sitting in a corner angled so that it reflected both the hall he was currently in and the hall he would be turning into in a moment. The glass's surface rippled as he came upon it, and a half-spear shot from it, piercing Harbin's calf. With a stifled scream, he pushed through the pain and began limping/running down the hall. In front of him was a single door leading to a room with a single candle within it. Harbin tried to imagine what Wyllran's plan was in this moment.

"Seeing the reflective surfaces set up throughout this hall, Lord Wyllran probably concluded that he needs a second reflection to move toward his destination... So what would happen if he suddenly had nowhere else to run?"

Harbin continued to push through the pain and kept running. In a flash, he barely managed to notice it in time as the reflected half-spear shot out from a silver sconce on the wall. He ducked, nearly collapsing on the ground altogether before forcing himself to get up and begin his mad dash once more.

"There's not even an exit here! HAHAHAH, what are you going to do now, you brat!?" The villain's cold voice retained its chill, however it seemed manic now.

Woosh!

This time, the spear flew through the air just barely missing Harbin's face before it hit another piece of glass on the other wall and disappeared within it. Then, in a surprising twist, that very same piece of glass suddenly flew into the middle of the hall as the fiend shouted out a truly terrible, pained shriek. Then the glass shattered into a dozen pieces in front of him. Each one floated in the air as he was reflected in each piece. Every single one of his reflections reached to their sides and pulled out a crossbow bolt. Then, in a swift motion, they simultaneously threw them like miniature javelins.

"ACK–!" Harbin reflexively exclaimed as he raised both of his arms to protect his head and chest. All at once, he felt as dozens of bolts pierced his skin. Many in his arms, his legs, his stomach, and his shoulders. However, not a single one hit a vital point and instead only brought him pain.

"You damn brat! Why won't you just DIE!?" The voice was now completely manic and full of anger. Its cold tone was no longer present as it seemed to be abandoning all caution to kill Harbin in any way it could.

Harbin pushed forward despite his wounds and dashed into the doorway to the room. There, he saw a singular candle atop a wooden stool resting in front of a floor-length mirror with a cloth piled on top of it.

The villain rushed forward, already appearing in the mirror's surface as Harbin quickly threw the door closed behind him.

The villain breathed heavily for a moment. His eyes were bleeding profusely, seemingly a side effect of the strain he had put upon his body with his attacks just moments before. "What now, boy!? You're here, all ALONE! In a room with only ME!"

Harbin shut his eyes, partially from fatigue and partially for what came next.

For the first time in his many years, Harbin did not wish to remain silent. "You mean you don't see it?"

The fiend looked around the room for a moment before responding. "WHAT!? Do you have a secret weapon hidden here!? Something you've found that you think could kill me!? I'M MUCH MORE IN-TELLIGENT THAN THAT BOY! WITHIN THIS REFLECTION, NO WEAPON CAN HARM ME! HAHAHAH!"

"No, not harm…" Harbin responded, his voice now turning just as cold as his enemy's had been many times before.

The voice became panicked, seemingly worried it had not ac-counted for something, as indeed…it had not.

"You didn't see the trap you've been placed in." Harbin walked for-ward, his hand hovering over the candle he knew was there even though his eyes remained tightly shut.

"What? no no no No NO!" The voice's panic increased as Harbin heard a dull thumping noise from where the mirror stood. He guessed that the fiend was attempting to break through as he had in the hall; however, he no longer had the energy to do so.

Harbin lowered his hand over the candle, feeling it begin to burn his skin. "Here is where you will remain for a long while."

"NO! Please! I'll spare you! I'll–!" His voice was cut off as Harbin pinched the candle wick, plunging the room into complete darkness, trapping the villain within this mirror, as he had nowhere left to es-cape to.

With a tired sigh, Harbin approached the mirror. He still did not dare to open his eyes as he carefully felt for the piece of cloth atop the fiend's new prison. With slow hands, he made sure that the fab-ric covered each and every bit of the reflective surface, not allowing anything else to be reflected within it. Then, with a resolute stride, he approached the doorway and opened it, sparing one glance over his shoulder before stepping through and closing it behind him.

The End